Rhiannon Lassiter

OXFORD
UNIVERSITY PRESS

Great Clarendon Street, Oxford OX2 6DP

Oxford University Press is a department of the University of Oxford.
It furthers the University's objective of excellence in research, scholarship,
and education by publishing worldwide in

Oxford New York

Auckland Cape Town Dar es Salaam Hong Kong Karachi
Kuala Lumpur Madrid Melbourne Mexico City Nairobi
New Delhi Shanghai Taipei Toronto

With offices in

Argentina Austria Brazil Chile Czech Republic France Greece
Guatemala Hungary Italy Japan Poland Portugal Singapore
South Korea Switzerland Thailand Turkey Ukraine Vietnam

First published 2006

British Library Cataloguing in Publication Data
Data available

ISBN 978-0-19-275487-5

3 5 7 9 10 8 6 4 2

Typeset by Newgen Imaging Systems (P) Ltd., Chennai, India
Printed in Great Britain by
Cox & Wyman, Reading, Berks.

Paper used in the production of this book is a natural,
recyclable product made from wood grown in sustainable forests.
The manufacturing process conforms to the environmental
regulations of the country of origin.

For Mo Holkar
'It's all about the pretext, baby!'

Contents

1. Minus One 1

2. Parallel Lines 23

3. Base Ten 45

4. The Nth Dimension 63

5. Zero Squared 89

1
Minus One

Multiplicity was one of the most exciting places to live in the world. Everything there was bigger or brighter or better than any other city. The skyscrapers were taller, the cars were faster, even the sky seemed bluer.

But most importantly, Multiplicity had the Hero Squad—its own super heroes. Captain Excelsior, Princess Power, and Animo had a base at the top of a skyscraper called Hero Heights and whenever the city was in trouble they'd come running, or flying, or with a herd of elephants—ready to save the day.

People said that Multiplicity must have its own arch villain as well. Someone must be responsible for all the cunning plans and evil schemes, and for commanding the criminals from behind the scenes. But the Hero Squad had never been able to find out who it was.

If they had, they might have been most interested in the news that Doctor Damian Void, respected scientist and renowned inventor, was leaving the city that very day in a spaceship of his own design.

Doctor D. Void waved goodbye to the watching crowd as cameras clicked, whirred, and flashed. He was amused that all the people cheering had no idea he was Multiplicity's secret arch villain.

As the doors of the spaceship slid shut he quickly went over to his big black chair facing a wall of computer screens and turned them on. Pressing buttons on his remote control he opened a transmission channel to his secret lair and one of the screens showed a muscled man with ginger hair sitting in an identical black chair.

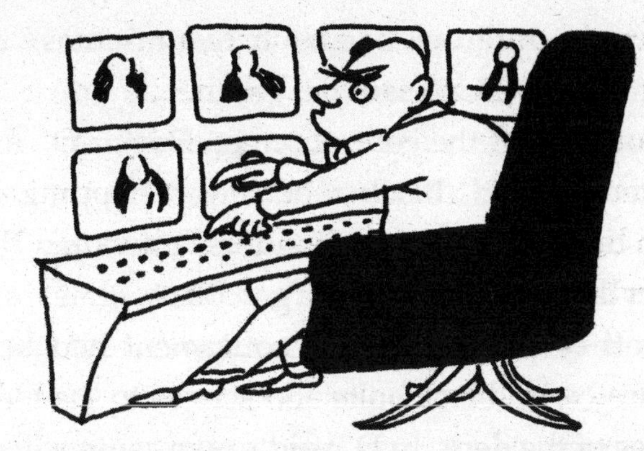

Doctor D. Void's spaceship was decorated, like his secret lair, in shades of black. The secret base also had a large number of white angora cats which shed fur over everything, but D. Void had been persuaded that cats would not enjoy the trip into space.

'The final preparations have been completed,' D. Void said. 'I will be away for at least six months. I expect you to keep up our criminal campaign against the city, Tench.'

'Yes, Doctor.' Terry Tench nodded. He was feeling excited and nervous about being left in charge. As a professional henchman he didn't often get the chance to make decisions. He was already day-dreaming about taking over the whole city before the doctor returned.

'The countdown begins in five minutes,' the doctor said. 'Don't fail me, Tench.'

Turning off the control screen Doctor D. Void looked around. Black robots were zipping up and down the black corridors, checking that everything was ready to go. Black crates and barrels of provisions and equipment had been secured with black bolts and screws to the black plates of the deck. In D. Void's own cabin a black bottle of champagne was chilling in a black ice bucket. All the same, something was missing.

'Jewel!' shouted the doctor. 'Where are you?'

Jewel was D. Void's daughter. She had long shiny black hair and brilliant green eyes and she wanted to be a scientist when she grew up. She certainly didn't want to be a super villain, or a villainess, or even a henchperson. Jewel thought villainy was a lot more trouble than it was worth.

As she lived in a secret lair, she hadn't got a lot of friends. Her best friend was Toby Tench, Terry Tench's son. She was using her video phone to say goodbye to him and she noticed he was looking excited. Toby always said Dr D. Void's plans were pretty pathetic and sometimes Jewel wondered if secretly he thought he could do a better job.

'I'm just happy for Dad,' Toby said, seeing that Jewel was frowning. 'This is a big opportunity for him.'

'A big opportunity to cause trouble,' Jewel said. 'Don't forget you're not a villain or a henchman, Toby. You're a Zero.'

The Zeroes were a secret club. Jewel and Toby were members. So were Ben, Pippa, and Marcus: the children of the Hero Squad. They'd made friends because they were all embarrassed by their parents and weren't impressed by fiendish schemes or daring deeds. The Zeroes weren't on the side of heroes or villains. Instead they supported all the people who didn't have special powers or wear costumes or stand out in any way.

'I know!' Toby said. 'Don't forget I'm starting at Ben's school next week. It's going to be great learning new things instead of just boxing and karate and how to salute.'

'I'm excited too,' Jewel admitted. 'I'll miss you all but we're going to be exploring space. I can't wait to find out what it's like.'

'Maybe you'll meet aliens,' Toby agreed.

In the background, a countdown began to boom through the ship:

'Lift-off in sixty seconds, fifty-nine, fifty-eight . . .'

Reaching for the off-button, Jewel said:

'I'd better go. Say goodbye to the others from me. I'll call again when we pass Pluto!'

On the other side of the city, the rest of the Zeroes were watching the spaceship-launch on television. A reporter was standing at the edge of the launch site.

'Today Doctor Damian Void and his daughter will be the first human beings to explore the solar system and the galaxy beyond,' said the reporter. *'Behind me you can see the spaceship Black Hole where the countdown has already begun. We go now to a direct link to the spaceship's computer pilot for the rest of that countdown.'*

They were in Pippa's bedroom and, as always, it was a mess. Pippa Power was a tomboy; she had short dirty-blonde hair and wore a grubby T-shirt and torn jeans. On her right hand was a pen and ink tattoo of a spider. Pippa loved sports and her room had piles of roller-skates and tracksuits and games everywhere.

Pippa lived in Power Towers. Recently the Towers had been damaged by a horde of rampaging robots and had needed to be rebuilt. There was still scaffolding outside. The old Power Towers had been pink from top to bottom. Pink used to be Princess Power's favourite colour. Luckily she'd changed her mind about that and now Power Towers was a shiningly bright white on the outside. The inside mostly hadn't been painted yet although Pippa's room was finished and now had black and purple striped walls.

'I'm glad your room was finished in time for us to watch the launch,' said Marcus, as the countdown continued on the huge TV screen. 'It's really cool. So your mum went off pink after all the trouble with the robots?'

'Yeah,' Pippa grinned. 'Even her hero costume's red now. But she still has a lot of pink dresses.'

'My dad's changed a bit too,' Marcus said, still keeping an eye on the screen. Marcus was small and asthmatic and wore glasses. A lot of things scared him, like animals and sports and anything large. This used to be a problem for him since his dad was Animo, a super hero who could control animals and who lived in the middle of his own private zoo. But during a crisis Marcus had shown his dad how good he was with computers and his dad had been so interested that now Marcus was starting to get more confident about everything in his life.

'He's stopped spending every day with the animals,' Marcus explained. 'He's even got his own computer now,' he added proudly. 'And I'm teaching him how to use it.'

Meanwhile the countdown was nearly over and Ben waved at the other two to be quiet.

'The spaceship's about to take off!' he said.

Ben was the leader of the Zeroes. This wasn't because his father was Captain Excelsior. It was because when the Zeroes first met Ben had more reason to hate heroes and villains than any of them. His dad was always so busy saving the world he didn't have much time for Ben. But he'd promised to change and this time Ben hoped it would be true.

'Eleven, ten, nine, eight, seven, six . . .'

The rockets that powered the ship rumbled, glowing yellow, then blue, then finally white hot. Leaning forward the Zeroes joined in the countdown.

'Five . . . four . . . three . . . two . . . one . . . ZERO!'

On the television they saw the rocket rise up from the ground and streak up into the sky, rising higher and higher until it was just a dot. On the ground the crowd were cheering and in Pippa's room the Zeroes joined in.

Turning off the television, Pippa grabbed a packet of crisps from the table and opened them so messily that fragments went all over the room.

'I can't believe Jewel's going to be gone for six months,' she said.

'She's so lucky,' Marcus said, sounding envious. 'Imagine all the things she'll see, like comets, and supernovas . . .'

'I'm just glad the ship took off safely,' Ben said, finally relaxing. 'You have to admit, not all Doctor D. Void's inventions work the way they're supposed to.'

The others nodded. It was true. Doctor D. Void's fiendish devices were sometimes just a little too fiendish for their own good. His robotic spiders had a tendency to climb up buildings and try to eat helicopters. His mechanical mole-men would dig huge holes and then sulk in the bottom. His mutants and monsters always oozed slime whether they were supposed to or not.

'Where's Toby?' Marcus asked and Pippa replied:

'He said he'd come as soon as he could.'

At that moment the door opened and they all turned to see a six-foot tall furry robot standing there. Poppet was one of Princess Power's assistants and up until recently it had been a bright pink. Now its fur was a snowy white, like a polar bear or a yeti.

'Your friend is here, Miss Pippa,' Poppet said in its high squeaky voice and stepped aside so that they could see Toby standing behind it.

'Hey, guys,' he said, grinning. He had brought a bag of snacks with him and he poured them out on to the table as he came to join them. 'Jewel said to say goodbye to you all and that she'd call on her way past Pluto.'

The Zeroes cheered again. But as they

quietened down there was a noise outside the window. It sounded as if it came from everywhere at once, a sort of whistling roar. They all looked at the window and then Marcus gasped and pointed.

'Look!' he said. High up in the sky was a small dot. But it was getting bigger. Something was falling through the air.

'Oh no.' Pippa ran to the window and opened it, climbing out on to the balcony and squinting up at the sky. The others joined her, all trying to see the object as it fell.

'Doctor D. Void does it again!' Marcus said.

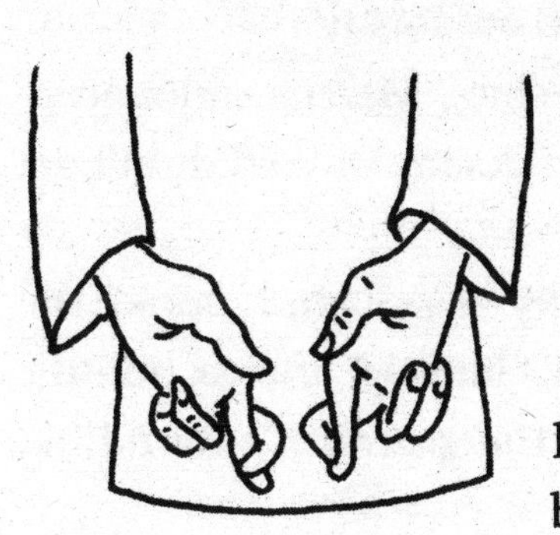

Ben didn't say anything. His fingers were crossed on both hands and his eyes were shut as he wished with all his heart that Jewel would be OK.

Out on the streets, people had also noticed the falling spaceship. Standing on corners and looking out of windows, they stared as it came plummeting down through the sky. Even for Multiplicity this was an unusual event and because they expected the Hero Squad to save the day no one wanted to stop watching.

On the balcony of Power Towers the Zeroes weren't quite as confident. They knew the Hero Squad could make mistakes. As the tiny dot got closer, Marcus grabbed a pair of binoculars from Pippa's room and tried to focus them on the spaceship. It was difficult because the ship was getting closer all the time, but finally he managed to get a fix on it and he gasped.

'What is it?' Ben said anxiously.

'It's a different spaceship!' Marcus announced. 'It's not the Black Hole. Doctor D. Void didn't get it wrong after all!'

'Let me see!' Toby said and took the binoculars. 'He's right,' he said after a minute. 'It's not black, for one thing. And it's round . . . like a flying saucer.'

'You mean it's aliens?' Pippa said excitedly. Although it was Marcus who liked computers Pippa had one as well which she mostly used for playing space invaders. Shading her eyes she stared up at the sky. The spaceship was much closer now and the whistling sound was changing into a hum. The windows of the skyscrapers rattled and shook as the noise seemed to come from everywhere at once.

'It's slowing down,' Marcus said.

He was right, the dot no longer seemed to be falling, instead it was hovering over the city and they could all see that it was a silver disc, shaped a little like a saucer.

'It's landing, you mean,' Ben said and he was right. From their vantage point, they could see the saucer getting lower and lower in the air, until it was hovering over Circle Square, one of the biggest open spaces in Multiplicity.

'Come on then!' Pippa said, excitedly. 'We can get there in ten minutes if we run. You don't want to miss aliens landing, do you?'

'That depends,' Marcus said thoughtfully. 'If they're invading, I wouldn't mind missing it.'

But Toby and Ben were already running after Pippa and, checking his inhaler was in his pocket, Marcus followed more slowly. He was as relieved as they were that Jewel's ship was all right but he didn't think aliens landing was anything to be pleased about. He'd played space invader games too and he knew the aliens always had the best weapons. Doctor D. Void had never managed to take over the city and Terry Tench wasn't likely to do any better, but space aliens sounded as if they might just manage it.

By the time the Zeroes reached Circle Square a crowd had gathered. This always happened in Multiplicity and normally the Zeroes just yawned. None of them were impressed by the Hero Squad's battles with mutants or machines or whatever D. Void had invented that week. But this time they had to push through the people to get a good view of where the saucer was still hovering just a couple of metres off the ground. Luckily, Toby was strong for his age and Pippa was tough but it took a while to get to the front of the crowd. Just as they were about to get into the front row Ben caught up with them and grabbed the back of Pippa's T-shirt to slow her down.

'Hold on,' he told them. 'Look who's coming.'

It was the Hero Squad. Looking up into the air they, and the rest of the crowd, could see three flying figures.

Captain Excelsior could fly and, as soon as he'd heard the news about the flying saucer, he'd gathered the rest of the Hero Squad and come straight to Circle Square. Now he posed on the top of a nearby skyscraper, waiting for the others to catch up. In his uniform and mask he looked brave and mysterious.

Princess Power had a rocket pack. This, like her costume, used to be pink. But now it was red, like her new jumpsuit, and a plume of red smoke followed her as she rocketed through the sky in a series of loops and swirls. The red smoke hung in the air for long enough for the people below to see she was spelling out words.

'Never fear, the Hero Squad are here,' Marcus read out, catching up with the others in time to see what was going on.

'She's such a show-off,' Pippa muttered, hiding behind a taller person in the crowd. If their parents spotted them, they'd probably be sent home and she'd miss all the excitement.

'They all are,' Marcus replied, spotting his dad.

Animo couldn't fly, but it didn't matter since he could speak with animals. A giant eagle was swooping through the sky with Animo hanging from a trapeze held in its claws. Heights didn't bother him and he was swinging back and forth on the trapeze and doing somersaults as the crowd cheered.

The Hero Squad landed in the square not far from the flying saucer and everyone went quiet, waiting to see what would happen. There was a loud hiss and from the middle of the saucer a ramp appeared, coming down to touch the paving stones. People held their breath as an eerie blue light shone out from the opening in the middle of the saucer.

Ben realized his fists were clenched. He wondered if he was the only one who remembered it wasn't the first time aliens had landed in Multiplicity. Ten years ago his father had just been an ordinary man called Keith

Carter. But he'd been unlucky enough to be visiting the city museum on the day an alien spaceship had arrived and squashed it flat. Keith had nearly died but the aliens hadn't meant to squash the museum, they'd only stopped to ask for directions and they'd apologized by rebuilding it and by giving Keith the special powers that had made him a super hero. That was all very well, but if they'd never come in the first place, Keith Carter would still just be an ordinary person. Ben was wondering if it was the same aliens this time and thinking about some of the things he'd like to say to space travelling busybodies who turned people's dad's into heroes without asking.

Toby was worried as well. His dad had only just been given his first chance to show that a henchman could run a lair of villains. What if these aliens were even more villainous than Doctor D. Void and tried to take over the city? Not only would the doctor be annoyed, he might blame Toby's dad for it. Even worse, what if they were heroes? Terry Tench might be able to hold his own against three super heroes, but if the aliens joined them he might be in serious trouble!

Pippa and Marcus were both squinting into the blue light. Pippa was wondering if the aliens were going to be oozing blobs or tentacled monstrosities and was rather hoping they would be both. Marcus was wondering the same thing and had his fingers crossed that they wouldn't be either. Around them the crowd whispered to each other as three shadowy figures appeared in the blue light and began to come down the ramp.

'They look human,' Marcus whispered, feeling relieved as he counted three people, each with the usual number of arms and legs and no tentacles whatsoever.

'Boring . . .' Pippa said, disappointed, but as the three figures marched down the ramp and faced the Hero Squad she was as fascinated as everyone else.

The aliens certainly looked human. The tallest figure was a man dressed in a blindingly white costume. He had a gold helmet that hid his face, a long golden cloak, and golden boots. It was an even more impressive costume than Captain Excelsior's and the man looked confident as he strode forward into the square.

The second figure was a woman. She had long

black hair and was wearing a blue jumpsuit that showed off her figure, but her face was hidden by a sapphire mask that glittered in the morning sunshine. People sometimes said that Princess Power was one of the most beautiful women in the world but, even with the mask, this woman might be the most beautiful in the galaxy.

The third was another man. He was wearing heavy metal armour that shone against his ebony skin. He had a metal visor over his eyes that displayed a shifting panel of coloured lights, like a computer screensaver. The lights were strangely hypnotic and the crowd's whispers hushed as he joined the other two.

The Hero Squad faced the newcomers and everyone wondered who would speak first. Captain Excelsior had just opened his mouth when the man in the white costume suddenly spoke in a voice that rang out across the square.

'Greetings, people of Earth and citizens of Multiplicity,' he said. 'We come in peace.'

There was a cheer from the crowd. People might enjoy seeing the Hero Squad fight villains, but these newcomers looked very confident and it was a relief to know they weren't planning to let loose with ray guns and laser beams in the city centre.

'I am General Excellence,' he said. 'And these are my companions, Quanta and Mesmeron. We are super heroes from a faraway planet and we have come to Multiplicity to invite your bravest men and women to join with us in an intergalactic group to fight villainy. You can call us the Infinity League!'

The other two, Quanta and Mesmeron, turned to wave at the crowd as they cheered again and even the Hero Squad clapped.

But the Zeroes weren't cheering. Pippa sniffed a bit as Quanta shook out her long black hair and blew kisses to the crowd.

'Just what we need,' she said, sarcastically. 'A group of even bigger show-offs than the Hero Squad.'

Marcus wasn't cheering either. The lights on

Mesmeron's visor were making him feel a bit queasy and he had to look away.

'Why do they have to wear masks?' he muttered. 'It's not as if anyone knows them here.'

'It's not as if anyone *wants* them here either,' Toby agreed angrily. 'How's my dad supposed to keep his job if there are six super heroes running around the city instead of three? It's not fair.'

'My dad was supposed to be spending the weekend with me,' Ben said sadly. 'I bet he won't have time now.'

It looked as if he was right. The Hero Squad were shaking hands with the Infinity League and it was obvious to everyone that they were inviting them to come to Hero Heights. The ramp closed up, leaving the saucer still hovering in the square. Then, as Captain Excelsior and the Hero Squad took off again, the Infinity League followed. General Excellence could fly as well as Excelsior could, Quanta's boots were rocket powered just like Princess Power's jet pack, and Mesmeron's armour hissed and whirred and then transformed into metal wings that lifted him into the air while Animo was still waiting for the eagle to return.

The crowd cheered again a couple of times and some of them hung around looking at the saucer, but it was clear the show was over. The Zeroes looked at each other rather glumly. A camera crew had arrived from one of the news stations and was still filming the disappearing figures of the heroes. A reporter was facing the camera and saying:

'. . . so on the very day the intrepid Doctor Damian Void sets off to explore the galaxy, the galaxy has come to us with an invitation for the Hero Squad to join in a daring new endeavour. Who knows what battles they'll be joining out in space . . .'

2

Parallel Lines

Meanwhile, Jewel knew nothing about aliens or the Infinity League. The starship Black Hole had only just passed the moon and was still accelerating. Doctor D. Void was having great fun using all his scanners to look for signs of alien life and cheerfully drinking the champagne.

Jewel had been allowed half a glass of champagne since it was a special occasion but she'd got bored with looking at the scanners and had gone instead to the observation room. This was right at the front of the spaceship where there was a window made of extra tough transparent titanium. Through this she could see the stars as the spaceship ploughed onwards facing away from the sun. Sitting on a black sofa, Jewel looked at the stars and daydreamed. She was wondering if they'd meet aliens and what they'd be like. Unlike Pippa and Marcus she wasn't thinking about tentacles but about strange alien languages. Perhaps she'd be the first to learn alien speech and find out about weird alien customs.

Unfortunately, right now there wasn't very much to see. Stars were much brighter out here but space itself was big and black and empty. It made Jewel feel a bit homesick. She and her dad were alone on the ship. Black robots whizzed up and down the corridors but you couldn't have a conversation with them. Doctor D. Void hadn't programmed them to talk and they just beeped at you if you got in their way. Even the cats back home had been better company although they were always yowling and scratching the furniture. Right now Jewel wouldn't have minded if one of them had jumped up into her lap and breathed fishy breath in her face while treading hard claws into her lap.

'Perhaps the aliens will have pets,' Jewel said to herself. 'Flying lizards or super intelligent fish or something like that. If they didn't have fur I could bring one back for Marcus.'

Thinking about presents for her friends cheered Jewel up a bit and she was wondering what she might be able to find for the others when she noticed something outside the window. Standing up, she went closer and stared out into the blackness, trying to work out what it was.

It was a sort of rippling ribbon of light. Looking at it made Jewel's eyes water but as she stared she realized that it didn't have an obvious beginning or an end. It looped and swirled through space like seaweed. It was hard to make out colours in the light. The longer she looked at it the harder it was for Jewel to decide if it was a warning red or a sickly green or an eerie blue. It seemed to change colour and shape in a way that hurt her eyes and gave her a headache.

Turning her back on it, Jewel hurried to the control room, dodging past whirring, beeping robots. When she got there Doctor D. Void was plotting their course on a map of the solar system and she could see the black shape that represented their spaceship was getting closer to Mars.

'There you are, Jewel,' her dad said. 'I was thinking about coming to join you. I want to take a closer look at those famous Martian canals.'

'Before you do,' Jewel said, 'have you noticed anything odd on the scanners? I thought I saw something out there . . .'

'Really? Something extraterrestrial?' Doctor D. Void looked excited and punched buttons on his computer console but after a moment he shook his head. 'Scanners don't detect anything unusual,' he said. 'Are you sure you didn't imagine it?'

'I don't think so,' Jewel replied. She had been daydreaming but she didn't think she could have imagined a strange swirling light like seaweed. But when they went back to the observation room together she had to admit there was no sign of the thing she'd seen. Up ahead was the red planet of Mars with its canal-shaped canyons that Doctor D. Void told her weren't actually canals at all.

'Your eyes can play tricks on you,' he told her. 'But I'll make a note of it in the log and we can have another look on the way back.'

Jewel nodded. She was still feeling worried about it. There was something she hadn't liked about that light. It had looked wrong, somehow. But she decided there wasn't anything she could do although she planned to mention it when she called the other Zeroes. Perhaps they'd have an idea about what it could be.

Toby was looking forward to talking to Jewel again. He wanted to warn her about the Infinity

League and ask whether she thought Doctor D. Void should be told. The other Zeroes were worried too but it was different for them. Their parents might be embarrassing but they were heroes. The city was on their side. It was different if your parents were villains, and Toby's weren't even important villains, just henchmen.

Saying goodbye to the others, he'd taken the bus back to Doctor D. Void's secret lair. The entrance was hidden in the basement of a carpark but Toby knew the secret code to get in. When he arrived he discovered that the corridors were bustling. Black-uniformed guards raced around, treading on white cats and getting in each other's way. Toby's mum and dad were in the main control room, watching repeats of the saucer landing on ten different news channels at once.

'Have you seen this?' his dad asked when Toby came in.

'More super heroes!' His mum pushed a cat out of the way of the screens so she could get a better view. 'That's the last thing we need.'

'I was there when they landed,' Toby told

them. 'They looked impressive. They can all fly, as well.'

They watched as the Hero Squad and the Infinity League took off together, heading for Hero Heights.

'Maybe this isn't such a bad thing,' Terry Tench said hopefully. 'If this Infinity League keeps the Hero Squad busy fighting crime somewhere out in space, we might actually stand a chance of taking over Multiplicity.'

'And what if these new heroes join in against us?' Tina Tench said. 'We're going to need to recruit a lot more villains to have a chance against them.'

'If only we knew what their plans were,' Toby said. 'I wonder what they've been saying to the Hero Squad.'

There was a soft cough behind them and Toby and his parents turned and looked. There was no one there. For a moment they stared blankly and then Terry Tench beamed.

'Fade!' he said. 'I'd forgotten all about you. Please tell me you've got some good news for us?'

It was easy to forget about the Fade, even though she was one of Doctor D. Void's most trusted agents. This was because she was invisible. The Fade could go anywhere without being noticed and this was what she'd been doing today.

'Not exactly good news,' a woman's voice said out of nowhere. 'But I have found out something . . .'

Toby and his parents listened intently as she explained.

The Fade had managed to sneak into Hero Heights at the same time as the Infinity League. While the Hero Squad were making them welcome and introducing themselves, she'd stood quietly in a corner out of the way and watched.

'General Excellence is the leader,' she said. 'And he's certainly confident. He said he's quashed arch villains in thirteen different solar systems and foiled nefarious plots in another twenty-five, although he was a bit vague on the details. Quanta let him do most of the talking but she was very friendly, especially to Excelsior and Animo.' The Fade sounded disapproving. 'She talked a lot about universal peace and love.'

'And the other one? Mesmeron?' Toby's dad asked and the Fade's voice sounded ominous.

'He only said one thing,' she told them. 'Most of the time he just sat and stared at the others. But at one point the Hero Squad asked some questions about what exactly the Infinity League did and Mesmeron stood up and looked at them behind that strange visor he has. He said "The Infinity League are heroes. Trust us". After that the Hero Squad seemed convinced. When I left they were arranging for Excellence, Quanta, and Mesmeron to have rooms in Hero Heights.'

'So they are moving in,' Terry Tench said miserably. 'I'd better start advertising for more villains. With three more heroes in town we're going to need more staff.'

'I'll get the latest batch of job applications,' Tina told him. 'I remember we had a few applicants looking for a dishonest day's wage. Mostly sidekicks and goons but we can't afford to be fussy.'

As they started making plans Toby felt a hand tap him on the shoulder and gently pull him aside. Leaving his parents behind he followed the Fade out of the room.

'Toby,' she said quietly. 'You know my secret, don't you?'

Toby nodded, and after a moment a woman appeared in the blank space in front of him. She had her red hair tied back in a long plait, but even so he recognized her. When the Zeroes had started a campaign against their own parents, heroes and villains alike, to stop them being so embarrassing, the Fade had been the only person to guess the truth. This was because she had a secret identity of her own. Her real name was Fay and she was Keith Carter's girlfriend. Toby had often wondered where her real loyalty lay; was she on Doctor D. Void's side or on Captain Excelsior's?

'I'm worried,' the Fade said softly. 'I know your dad thinks this is bad news for villainy. But I think it might be even worse news for the Hero Squad. After all, we don't have any proof that the Infinity League are good. Whatever Mesmeron says.'

'You said that when he told the heroes to trust him, they seemed convinced,' Toby said thoughtfully. 'I wonder what his special power is . . .'

'That's what I wondered too,' the Fade said. 'Remember, he didn't know I was there so he wasn't looking at me but he looked at each of the Hero Squad for a long time and I could see strange coloured lights on his visor. Do you know what mesmerism is, Toby?'

Toby thought about it. The word did seem familiar. Suddenly the answer clicked and he nodded.

'It's a kind of hypnotism, isn't it?' he said. 'You think he was hypnotizing the Hero Squad?'

'I'm afraid so,' the Fade whispered. 'And if I'm right . . .'

'If you're right the Infinity League aren't heroes at all,' Toby realized. 'They're villains. And they're trying to take over the city without a fight!'

Ben was already sick of the Infinity League. Just as he'd suspected, his dad had called off their plans for the weekend. So instead of visiting his dad's flat and having take-away food and watching films Ben was sitting in the living room in his mum's house watching the news and sulking. All anyone could talk about was the Infinity League even though no one actually knew anything about them.

'Since they arrived in a flying saucer it's only reasonable to assume they have an advanced form of space travel capability,' one of the reporters was saying. *'But we don't yet know where the League is based or the significance of the word "infinity".'*

Ben turned off the television crossly. He knew what infinity meant, they'd studied it in maths last term. Infinity was the biggest number there could possibly be, it was so big it couldn't be counted. The sign the League had on their uniforms meant infinity: a twisted loop without a beginning or an end.

Ben picked up the video phone and punched in Marcus's number.

Marcus was sitting in his bedroom when he answered the phone. He looked almost as miserable as Ben felt.

'Did your dad cancel plans with you too?' Ben asked when he saw him, and Marcus nodded.

'He said Mesmeron was going to show him a more efficient way to use the Hero Heights computer system. I was the one who showed him how to use it in the first place!'

'My dad cancelled on me as well,' Ben said. 'I thought we were getting on better now. But when he called he didn't sound sorry. All he could talk about was the Infinity League and how important it was.'

'That's all anyone can talk about,' Marcus said. 'Mum thinks it's great. She was worried that Dad wasn't getting enough recognition for all he does. She thinks being asked to join an intergalactic crime fighting force is really cool.'

'What about Pippa?' Ben asked. 'Have you heard from her?'

'She's here,' Marcus said. 'Hey, Pippa, do you want to speak to Ben?'

'In a minute!'

Ben heard Pippa's voice and Marcus moved the phone so that he could see her as well. She was playing space invaders on Marcus's computer, controlling a tiny ship that was shooting rows and rows of invading aliens. There was a fierce grin on her face and she hunched over the controller, pressing buttons furiously.

'Hi, Ben,' she said when the last wave of aliens had vanished from the screen. 'My mum ditched me as well. She says Quanta's teaching her how to use rocket-powered boots instead of a jet pack.'

'Any idea how long they're going to stay for?' Ben asked and Pippa made a face.

'I bet they stay for months and months,' Marcus said miserably.

'They can't!' Ben said. 'It was bad enough Dad saving Multiplicity every day, if he's supposed to go out and save the galaxy once a week as well, I'll never see him!'

'But what can we do?' Marcus asked. 'Dad would be really disappointed if he couldn't join. This is a big opportunity for him.'

'For Mum too,' Pippa agreed. 'Captain Excelsior's always been the leader. Being part of the Infinity League would give Mum something more to do. And she says General Excellence is fantastic . . .'

Ben looked at his friends and tried to think of something to cheer them up. He couldn't think of anything. Just then he saw a light on the phone blinking and he realized someone else was trying to contact him.

'Hang on a minute, it's Toby.' He pressed buttons so that on one side of the screen he saw Marcus and Pippa and on the other Toby's freckled face. 'Hi, Toby,' he said. 'Have you been watching the news?'

'My parents have,' Toby said and for a moment Ben expected him to add that they'd been ignoring him as well. But instead he continued: 'But that's not important. The Fade was here earlier and she told me something you guys need to know about.'

'What?' Ben asked. 'Just a minute, I'll connect you to Marcus and Pippa as well.'

Toby waited until they were all listening and then said importantly:

'The Fade thinks the Infinity League are evil!'

Marcus and Pippa exchanged glances and then both suddenly grinned and Pippa gave Marcus a high five.

'Really?' Ben asked. 'That's fantastic!'

'It is?' Toby looked confused. 'Zeroes! This is serious. The Fade saw the Infinity League hypnotize the Hero Squad to make them believe they're trustworthy.'

'That is serious,' Ben said, calming down. 'But we were all worried about the League anyway. This gives us a reason to do something about them.'

'But if they're being hypnotized, our parents won't listen if we tell them this,' Pippa pointed out.

'Then we'll just have to do something ourselves,' Marcus insisted.

'Why don't we start by investigating their flying saucer?' Ben suggested. 'They've just left it in Circle Square.'

'It probably has all sorts of security systems,' Toby told them. 'Any self-respecting super villain always does. We have lots at Doctor D. Void's lair.'

'Then you'll have had lots of practice getting past them, won't you?' Ben said and Toby grinned.

'I'll meet you guys in half an hour,' he said. 'Ask your parents if you can go and see a film at the Multiplex, that's only five minutes from the square.'

Ben said goodbye quickly and went to ask his mum if he could go and meet Toby at the cinema.

Since she knew how disappointed he was not to be seeing his dad that night she said yes and agreed to drive him there. Five minutes after they left the house his phone starting beeping again. This time there was no one to answer it.

Out in space Jewel put down the phone disappointedly. There was no answer from Ben's house either. At Power Towers the white furry robot named Poppet had told her both Pippa and the Princess were out. At Animo's zoo his wife had answered and said Pippa and Marcus had been there but they'd gone out to another friend's house earlier. At the secret lair Toby's phone had just rung and rung until a henchman in black answered it and told her politely that Toby had gone to a karate class.

Jewel felt lonely. It sounded as if all her friends were having plenty of fun without her. Meanwhile, space wasn't as interesting as she'd expected it to be. Outside the window of her cabin she could see Pluto disappearing behind them. It was just a ball of rock. It had a moon, but that was another slightly smaller ball of rock.

Compared to Jupiter, Saturn, and Neptune it just wasn't exciting at all.

'And Pluto's the last planet as well,' she said to herself. 'After that . . .' She stopped as she realized that she didn't actually know what came after that. But her dad would know. Jewel went to look for him.

She found Doctor D. Void in the observation room drinking a cup of tea. He smiled as she came in and said thoughtfully, 'Tea tastes quite different in space. You know, I think I'd actually got used to having it full of cat hair.'

'I miss the cats too,' Jewel said. Looking past the doctor and through the window she could see small scattered pieces of rock here and there in space.

'We're still in the Kuiper Belt,' her dad told her, seeing where she was looking. 'It's basically an area of floating space debris.'

'More lumps of rock then,' Jewel said and the doctor looked surprised.

'Yes, but fascinating ones,' he said enthusiastically. 'They go on until we reach the Kuiper Gap. That's when things get really interesting.'

'They do?' Jewel said hopefully.

'Yes. You see, as far as anyone knows there's nothing out there,' the doctor explained. 'Just miles and miles of empty space.'

'That doesn't sound very interesting,' Jewel said doubtfully.

'Well, perhaps you'll find the Oort Cloud more exciting,' the doctor suggested. 'That comes after the Gap. It's a cloud of comets.'

'Lots and lots of tiny balls of rock,' Jewel said. She wasn't trying to be difficult but space had become very predictable and she was missing her friends.

Before her father could reply one of the black robots zoomed into the room, wheels spinning as it screeched to a halt and began beeping.

'What's up?' Jewel asked. 'It sounds as if it's blown a fuse.'

'I don't know,' Doctor D. Void put his tea down and stood up. 'I told all the robots to watch different parts of the controls and to come and find me if there was a problem. But I don't know which one this is.'

Jewel rolled her eyes. All her dad's inventions were like this. They worked just fine right up until there was a problem he hadn't expected and then they were worse than useless.

'We'd better go to the control room then,' she said.

The robot seemed to want them to follow. Whirring and beeping it led them back along the black corridors, through the black doors, and into the black control room. Once they were there, Doctor D. Void went to the only control panel that didn't have a robot in front of it and started pressing buttons.

'The scanner's picked up something out there, an unidentified object in the Kuiper Gap.' He pressed some more buttons and an image came to life on one of the screens. It showed the ship as a small glowing shape at the bottom of the screen, surrounded by tiny dots that symbolized the rocks around them. The middle of the screen was empty, just as D. Void had said it would be. But up at the top of the screen was a large round shape, much bigger than the ship.

'What's that?' Jewel asked and her dad grinned fiendishly.

'There's only one thing it can be,' he said. 'It's a new planet.'

Suddenly he jumped up from the chair and began to march up and down, waving his arms as he always did when he was especially excited.

'A tenth planet! One no one's ever spotted before!' His eyes flashed with delight. 'I'll claim it in the name of villainy, build a space base and create armies of robots to conquer the Earth. Eventually the whole universe will know the name of D. Void . . .'

Jewel usually tried to ignore her father when he got on to one of his 'I'll Show Them' speeches. But this time even she was excited. However, she was wise enough to know that not everything turned out the way her father expected it to.

'Hadn't we better go and look at it then?' she said. 'And find out what this planet you've discovered is actually like?'

'Good idea.' Doctor D. Void turned to the robots and started giving orders, telling them to set a course for the planet. Jewel hardly heard him, or the whistling beeps that answered him. She was looking at the screen again and grinning to herself. Finding a new planet would be something to tell her friends back home.

3
Base Ten

Ben's mum dropped him off in front of the Multiplicity Multiplex, the largest cinema in the city. He could already see Pippa and Marcus waiting outside and waving to him.

'I'll pick you up in two hours,' his mother said. 'What film are you going to see?'

'Um, it's about spies,' Ben said quickly. 'Thanks, Mum. See you later.'

Jumping out of the car he ran to meet the others and they all waved as his mum's car pulled back into the stream of traffic and left. The moment she was gone they turned their backs on the cinema and set off for Circle Square.

'Mum's coming to pick me up in two hours,' Ben said. 'We'll have to work fast.'

Pippa nodded. She looked ready for action.

'I'm not sure this is such a great idea,' Marcus said uncertainly.

He was holding his inhaler as if he thought he might need it any moment and looking left and right nervously.

When they got to Circle Square, Toby was waiting for them. He was dressed in black and he was wearing a heavy utility belt around his waist and carrying a rucksack.

'You made it,' he said, coming up to join them. 'I've been watching the flying saucer for a while and there doesn't seem to be anyone guarding it.'

The flying saucer was still where they had last seen it, hovering a couple of metres above the ground. There was no sign of the ramp that had lowered before and Ben hoped Toby would have a good plan for getting them inside.

Five minutes later he was having some doubts.

'Hurry up, you guys!' he said. 'I'm not sure how long I can do this . . .'

'You can talk,' Toby grunted. 'I'm carrying the whole weight!'

'I still say I should be on the top,' Pippa complained. 'Get on with it, Marcus!'

'It's harder than it looks, OK,' Marcus snapped. He was having trouble keeping his balance. One hand was holding an electronic skeleton key that Toby said would open any lock. The other was clinging to Pippa's short hair as he sat on her shoulders. Beneath him, Pippa was holding on to his legs as she stood on Ben. Ben was standing on Toby's shoulders and feeling as if his arms were about to fall off. At the very bottom of the pyramid Toby was feeling grateful for all his karate, boxing, and judo lessons. Even so he was finding it quite difficult to support all the weight.

'It wouldn't hurt you lot to do some exercise once in a while,' he said. 'Or this wouldn't be so difficult!'

'Just tell me how to use this key!' Marcus hissed in a furious whisper. 'There's no keyhole or anything!'

'It's *electronic,*' Toby said. 'You just touch it to the door and press the button!'

There was a sudden buzzing noise and then a door sprang open in the bottom of the saucer and a ramp dropped down. Marcus flinched and let go of the skeleton key, clinging with both hands to Pippa's head.

'Owch,' Pippa yelled, losing her grip on Marcus's legs and beginning to wobble.

'Look out!' Ben cried as he felt himself falling.

As the ramp descended the Zeroes found themselves in a pile on the ground next to it. Gradually untangling themselves and rubbing bruised arms and legs, they looked at the ramp and the open door.

'Well, it worked,' Toby said.

'I think you've been spending too much time with Doctor D. Void,' Ben grumbled. 'I wouldn't exactly say that was a plan that *worked*.'

'We got in, didn't we?' Pippa pointed out. 'Come on, let's see what's inside.'

'Maybe someone should keep watch,' Marcus said. 'In case the Infinity League come back . . .'

'Good idea,' Ben said, thinking Marcus could probably do with a break. One of the lenses of his glasses was cracked and he was looking rather pale.

It was already getting dark and the door of the saucer was glowing with an eerie blue light. As Toby and Pippa headed up the ramp Ben followed them, looking back once to give Marcus a thumbs up.

In space there's no such thing as day and night. But everyone has to sleep sometimes. It would be hours until they arrived at the planet and Doctor D. Void thought they might as well get some rest. But in her cabin, tossing and turning, Jewel couldn't seem to get to sleep. She was still wide awake an hour after she'd gone to bed, even though her eyelids were heavy and she felt exhausted.

The bed in her cabin faced a small round

window, like the porthole of a ship, and she watched sleepily as the odd rock tumbled past and then there was nothing. They'd passed the Kuiper Gap and beyond this point there was nothing between them and the mysterious planet. At least there shouldn't be . . .

Jewel blinked and sat up, rubbing her eyes. She'd seen something, something strange. Pressing her face to the window she stared out at the blackness. For a long time there was nothing and she was feeling sleepy by the time she saw it again: the twisted ribbon of light made up of all colours at once. It coiled through space like a poisonous snake and just looking at it made Jewel feel queasy. She hadn't imagined it after all. Watching through the window she wondered what it could possibly be, since it hadn't shown up on any of the ship's scanners or sensors. She was still worrying when she lay down and finally fell into a deep sleep.

When they woke up it looked from the radar screens in the control room as if the Black Hole was just a few centimetres away from the planet. The robots were whizzing about from control panel to control panel and Doctor D. Void was muttering to himself and looking anxiously at the screen.

'There you are,' he said, as Jewel came in. 'I was worried you might miss it. We're almost there. I'm about to program a landing. You'd better strap yourself in.'

Jewel quickly took a seat in one of the big black chairs and put on the seatbelt. Her father was already wearing his. Putting his hands on the steering controls he looked around and said, 'Ready?'

'Yes, Dad.' Jewel nodded. Then she realized something. 'Um, hadn't you better . . .'

But it was too late. Doctor D. Void had already pulled the lever that began the landing and the ship had started to tilt. Strapped into their chairs Jewel and her dad weren't affected by the movement but the robots didn't have the same advantage. Their wheels skidded and screeched on the smooth black floor as they all started to roll down to one end of the room, beeping loudly to each other.

'Straighten the ship out!' Jewel called out but the doctor shook his head.

'I can't,' he said. 'We're already too close.'

Beeps and crashes sounded all around them as the robots collided with the wall and fell over, their wheels spinning helplessly. The whole ship hummed as the engines slowed and they entered the planet's atmosphere. On the screen Jewel could see it getting closer and closer as the beeps and whirrs got louder. She closed her eyes and put her hands over her ears but she could still feel the ship shaking. Then there were a whole series of banging sounds and the ship bounced and rattled, and then finally, silence.

Jewel opened her eyes and saw Doctor D. Void looking pleased. He took his hands off the controls and undid his seatbelt.

'We're down,' he said. 'A perfect landing.'

Jewel looked at the pile of battered robots beeping softly and sadly to themselves and wondered how her dad managed to ignore the facts. Already he was getting out two spacesuits and putting his on.

'Good job, Dad,' she said. After all, they were both still in one piece, which probably counted as a success. Undoing her own straps she went and helped the robots pick themselves up. Their pepper-pot shape meant that they couldn't do much on their own. They whirred gratefully as she got them upright again.

'Hurry up, Jewel,' D. Void said, handing her a spacesuit. He was still pretending the incident with the robots hadn't happened. 'Aren't you excited to see your first glimpse of a brand new world?'

Putting on the suit she'd been given, Jewel nodded to show she was ready.

'Don't take off your helmet,' Doctor D. Void warned her. 'The air might not be safe to breathe.'

As they went to the main doors of the ship, he could hardly contain his impatience. He was fidgeting as the doors slowly opened and as soon as there was enough room he had pushed through them and was out. Following more slowly, Jewel saw that they were standing on a grey rocky slope. Above them the sky was a pale grey as well.

Doctor D. Void was gazing out across the grey landscape and through the face-plate of his helmet Jewel could see he was looking proud.

'As the first person to discover this planet,' he said, 'I shall name it . . .'

'Um, Dad.' Jewel tugged on the sleeve of the doctor's suit. 'I don't think you are the first person to discover it, after all.'

'What?' The doctor frowned at her interruption and gently Jewel turned him around to look in the other direction.

'See,' she said. 'If we're the first, who built *that*?'

The doctor's mouth dropped open as he saw what she had seen.

In the middle of the grey rocky landscape was a huge white building. It faced the black shape of the spaceship from across the valley. Doctor D. Void gave it a long hard look. Then he started walking.

'I don't know who built it,' he said, 'but I'm going to find out!'

Meanwhile, back on Earth, the rest of the Zeroes were exploring the flying saucer. Luckily the skeleton key hadn't broken when it hit the ground, since most of the doors inside were locked. But the inside of the saucer was disappointing. There were lots of computer systems marked with signs that read 'power generator', 'stardrive', or 'hover control'.

'Don't touch anything,' Toby warned when he saw Pippa getting a bit too close. 'If we accidentally turn off the hover control or something the saucer might crash.'

'No bad thing if it did,' Pippa said. 'It'd serve them right for hypnotizing Mum.'

'Don't forget Marcus is underneath it,' Ben reminded them. 'If the saucer crashes it'll squish him flat.'

'Good point.' Pippa put her hands behind her back.

'We should look for the main control room,' Toby said. 'Doctor D. Void always keeps a record of his fiendish plans. If the Infinity League do the same we might be able to find out what they're up to.'

But the next room they found wasn't a control room. It looked more like someone's bedroom. There were photographs and newspaper articles taped all over it, so many that you could hardly see the walls. All the photographs were of people in costume and all the articles had headlines like 'Heroes Save The Day'.

'This looks like something one of the kids at my school would do,' Ben said, puzzled. 'Someone who was really keen on super heroes.'

'Look, there's a picture of Mum,' Pippa pointed out, going to take a closer look. 'I remember when this was taken, she's still wearing her old pink costume.'

'But there are lots of these I don't recognize,' Toby said. 'I didn't think there were this many super heroes in the whole world.'

'This one looks a bit like my dad,' Ben said, showing the others a poster of a hero with bulging muscles and a brilliant white smile. 'It says Commander Extreme, though.'

'And this one looks like Marcus's dad,' Pippa

said. She was looking at a photograph of a strong black man next to a lion, in one of the newspaper cuttings. 'But the article says he's called the Zookeeper.'

'Perhaps it's just a coincidence,' Toby suggested. 'But it does look awfully like him.'

'Maybe these are other heroes the League's planning to hypnotize?' Ben said.

'Or ones they've met and hypnotized already,' Pippa said grimly.

'But we still don't know what all of this is for,' said Toby. 'Why are the Infinity League collecting details of all sorts of different heroes?'

The Zeroes looked at each other. None of them could make any sense of it. But just as Toby was about to suggest they move on, they heard the sound of footsteps in the corridor. Someone was coming.

Toby and Pippa looked around the room for anywhere they could hide and, finding nowhere, they bunched their fists up, ready to fight. But Ben went quietly to the door of the room and opened it a crack, peering out.

'It's Marcus!' he realized and opened the door the whole way. 'Marcus, over here!'

Marcus couldn't say a word when he joined them. He was out of breath and panting.

'What is it?' Toby asked impatiently. 'Did you see something outside?'

Marcus nodded and sucked down another couple of breaths.

'They're coming!' he said finally. 'I saw them come flying down . . .'

'Who're coming?' Pippa looked wildly down the corridor. 'The Infinity League?'

'Not just them,' Marcus told them. 'The Hero Squad too! You've got to get off the saucer!'

Ben started running and the others followed, Marcus bringing up the rear as they dashed back to the doorway and the ramp. But by the time they got there it was too late. They could see General Excellence, Quanta, and Mesmeron in the distance, flying towards the saucer, with the Hero Squad following.

Quickly Toby touched the skeleton key to the panel by the door and the ramp lifted back up, shutting them into the saucer.

'Why did you do that?' Pippa asked. 'Now we can't get out!'

'But with any luck they won't know we're

here,' Ben said. 'Come on, we'd better find somewhere to hide . . .'

It took Jewel and Doctor D. Void some time to reach the gleaming white building and by the time they got there the doctor was extremely cross. He'd been muttering to himself as they walked and Jewel felt sorry for him. Her father might have his flaws, like being a villain and being obsessed with black, and the way that very few of his inventions ever worked the way they were supposed to, but all the same she was fond of him and sorry to see him upset.

The entrance to the white building was through a huge metal doorway with a complicated-looking computer-lock outside. Doctor D. Void looked at it for a minute and then pressed some buttons and the door opened. Inside, a long white corridor wound away into the distance, with bright white lights fixed at intervals along the ceiling.

'It looks like your secret lair, Dad,' Jewel said. 'Only white instead of black.'

'Hmmph.' Doctor D. Void looked annoyed. 'I don't see the similarity.'

Jewel kept quiet as they went through the door and started walking along the corridor. They hadn't gone far when they came to a fork in the path. As they were standing there deciding which way to go, a white robot, shaped a bit like a salt cellar, came whizzing along one of the corridors and had to brake when it neared them. It spun its wheels, beeped a bit, and then took off along the other corridor.

'Doesn't that remind you of anything?' Jewel asked and Doctor D. Void looked deliberately blank.

'No,' he said. 'Nothing at all.'

It was actually a bit creepy, Jewel thought. The heavy boots of her spacesuit echoed down the passageway. Occasionally there was a beep or a whirr as a robot passed them but no sign of any human life.

'There must be someone here,' she said eventually. 'Someone's got to be controlling the robots.'

'Someone must have built this . . . this *place,*' Doctor D. Void said. 'And when I find out who they are I'm going to give them a piece of my mind.' He continued ranting for a while as they walked. Jewel found it less annoying than usual—at least it was a sound she recognized.

Then, suddenly, the corridor came to an end, opening out into a huge room with a transparent ceiling through which they could see the starry sky. All around the room were computer consoles with robots working at them and there was a strange machine shaped like a cage in the middle of the room with red warning signs around it. But the most bizarre thing was the walls. They were completely covered in writing.

Looking closer Jewel realized that most of the writing was numbers. It started on a large whiteboard but had ended up overlapping the edges and spiralling around the walls. It looked as if someone had started doing a difficult sum and had run out of space for it. Jewel was good at maths and science but even she felt overwhelmed by the number of equals signs and plus signs and all sorts of other signs she didn't even recognize. The sum trailed off in so many directions it was almost impossible to see where it ended. But on the opposite wall one of the signs was larger than any of the others. It looked something like a twisted zero.

As Jewel stared at it she recognized it for what it was: an infinity symbol. But, before she could mention it, a man walked into the room.

He was very tall and thin, dressed in a white lab-coat and wearing thick glasses. He was muttering something to himself as he entered and tugging frustratedly at his wild white hair. He didn't see them and Doctor D. Void had to attract his attention.

'You over there!' the doctor called out. 'I'm Doctor D. Void, scientist, explorer, and many other things besides. Who on earth are you?'

'I'm Professor N. Vention,' the man told them, in a cross voice. 'And we're not on Earth. This is Planet X. What are you doing here?'

4

The Nth Dimension

Doctor D. Void and Professor N. Vention didn't exactly hit it off. The doctor was annoyed to discover someone already living on the planet he thought he'd discovered. The professor wasn't pleased to find that someone had landed a spaceship on the planet he claimed was his. Jewel did her best to explain:

'I'm sorry we just walked in but when we found the planet we were really excited,' she said, trying to flatter the professor. 'We're exploring the universe, you see.'

'Just the universe?' Professor Vention didn't look impressed at all.

'What do you mean, *just* the universe?' Doctor D. Void demanded. 'It's the *universe*, it's everything there is!'

Professor Vention looked smug. Jewel recognized the expression. It was the same one her father had when he'd come up with a particularly cunning plan and had to tell someone about it.

'There's more than one universe,' Professor Vention told them. 'This is just the one you know. I've personally visited over fifty different universes and I didn't need a spaceship to do it either. I've invented a way of travel that's far more advanced.'

Jewel smiled to herself. Her father liked to call himself an arch villain but he didn't mind being called an evil genius. However he got annoyed if anyone referred to him as a mad scientist. Professor Vention, on the other hand, was definitely a mad scientist, you just had to look at the mathematical equations that he'd written all over his walls. She wasn't surprised when he started to explain his equipment to them.

'We're standing in the middle of my device right now,' Professor Vention continued. 'When the Infinity machine is turned on this entire planet moves from one universe to the next.' He began to laugh, a crazy look in his eyes.

Doctor D. Void and Jewel exchanged glances. They were fascinated despite themselves.

'What are the other universes like?' Jewel asked.

Professor Vention finally stopped laughing and went back to looking irritated.

'Not that different from this one,' he said in a lecturing tone of voice. 'In the last one, I visited a version of Earth where the sea was green and the grass was blue but otherwise it's much the same as this. Even the countries have the same sort of names and the people too. In fact if you travelled to another universe you'd probably meet a version of yourself.'

'Another version of me?' Doctor D. Void sounded extremely interested. 'I wonder if we'd get on with each other?'

'I wonder,' Jewel said. She was thinking hard.

Professor Vention wasn't exactly brilliant company. He kept bursting into fits of laughter, or rushing off to scribble an addition to one of the equations or adjusting something on the controls.

Doctor D. Void wanted to know more about the secrets of travelling across the Multiverse and Jewel was wondering if there was a link between Planet X and the strange swirling seaweed-like lights she'd seen in space. Something about the looping equations had reminded her of them.

'Professor,' her dad suggested after a while, 'why don't you come back to our ship and tell us some more about your fascinating theories?'

'They're not theories, they're facts,' the professor snapped. 'And I can't possibly spare the time.'

'But your machine looks as if it's built already,' Jewel said. 'Don't you get lonely?'

Suddenly Professor Vention looked glum. He stopped cackling to himself and started tearing his hair again.

'The robots aren't much company,' he said, and Jewel heard a couple of robots make offended trills of noise.

'Mine aren't either,' Doctor D. Void agreed. 'Luckily I have Jewel to talk to.'

'I've got a daughter her age back home,' Professor Vention said, frowning. 'Her name's Gemma. But she's very judgemental. She absolutely refused to come with me when I told her about my plan.'

'That's a pity,' Doctor D. Void said. 'Look, why don't you come back and have lunch with us? I can show you around the Black Hole.'

As Professor Vention went to get his own spacesuit, Jewel and the doctor put their helmets back on. Jewel still wasn't sure what she thought about the professor but she was keen to get back to the ship. There was a phone call she wanted to make before lunch.

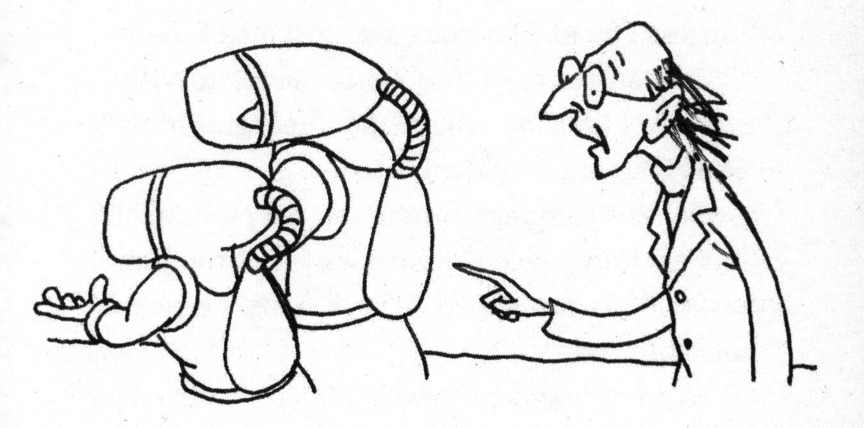

* * *

The other Zeroes would have liked to be able to make a phone call as well. Ben was kicking himself for having left his video phone behind. All four of them were squeezed behind a piece of machinery on the Infinity League's flying saucer, listening as footsteps came up the ramp towards the door.

The first person to speak was a woman and Pippa recognized her mum's voice.

'I'm sorry you have to leave so soon,' Princess Power said. 'I hope it won't be long before we see you again.'

'Likewise, I'm sure,' said another female voice. This time it was Quanta. Listening, the Zeroes realized that she sounded a lot like Princess Power. Her voice was just a bit huskier.

'Do you have a lot of other heroes to visit?' Captain Excelsior asked. Ben recognized his father's strong confident voice.

'No, as it happens, you're the last on our list.' General Excellence sounded just as strong and confident as he replied. 'The Infinity League is now complete.'

'So what happens next?' Marcus realized it

must be his dad, Animo, speaking. But when Mesmeron replied, he could hardly tell the difference.

'Now we go back to our own planet, until there's an emergency that requires our help,' Mesmeron told them. 'Just make sure that when your special Infinity alarm goes off, you go immediately to the Universal Equalizer.'

Behind the machinery the Zeroes looked at each other. They were puzzled by this.

'Universal Equalizer?' Pippa mouthed. The others shrugged or shook their heads.

It was difficult for the Zeroes, knowing that whatever the Infinity League were planning, they'd almost certainly lied to the Hero Squad. They were all tempted to jump out from behind the machinery and announce the truth. But not only would it be impossible to explain what they were doing there, it would be awful if their parents didn't believe them. Toby was the most worried of all. His dad might just be a henchman but technically that made him a villain. Even if the Hero Squad did believe their children, they wouldn't be likely to trust someone if they found out his dad worked for an arch villain.

The Infinity League were shaking hands and saying goodbye to the Hero Squad. It sounded as if they were planning to leave immediately and the Zeroes crossed their fingers, hoping they'd be able to get off the saucer before it was too late.

'Before you go,' Captain Excelsior said, 'I was wondering . . . Even though we helped you build the Universal Equalizer, I'm still not exactly clear on how it's supposed to work.'

There was a pause and then there was a weird flashing light. The Zeroes couldn't see where it was coming from but they could guess. Mesmeron was using his hypnotic power.

'You must trust the Infinity League.' Mesmeron's voice was calm and soothing. Even the Zeroes found it hard not to believe him. *'The Universal*

Equalizer will bring you to Infinity. When you hear the alarm you must stand on the platform and wait for the coloured light to surround you. Trust the Infinity League.'

'That makes sense.' Captain Excelsior's voice was relaxed. He didn't sound worried any more. Princess Power and Animo sounded the same as they said their final goodbyes.

As the Hero Squad trooped off back down the ramp, the Zeroes heard the door close behind them.

'Will they do it?' General Excellence said. He didn't sound friendly any more. Instead his voice was hard and cold.

'They're idiots.' Quanta sounded cruel and mocking. 'They'll do it all right.'

'They were completely hypnotized,' Mesmeron said. 'They'll do as I ordered.'

'And then . . .' Quanta said.

'Infinity will triumph!' said General Excellence.

The Zeroes listened intently as they heard the three villainous heroes walk off down the corridor.

'I think they've gone,' Ben whispered, finally

daring to move a muscle. But as he spoke he felt a hand come down on his shoulder. He froze in fright and heard a voice speak softly:

'What are *you* doing here?'

Doctor D. Void was obviously pleased to be able to show off his spaceship. It might not travel from universe to universe but it travelled through space just fine. Luckily the black robots had managed to repair themselves enough to ensure that the bumps and lumps weren't obvious.

By the time the three of them sat down to lunch, the doctor and the professor were getting on a lot better.

'I'm glad you could join us, Professor,' the doctor said, mixing the mad scientist a drink with a large helping of truth serum from a bottle labelled 'tonic water'.

'Call me Nicholas,' Professor Vention replied, smiling like a shark. 'So, Doctor, what is it you do when you're not exploring space?'

'Well.' Jewel could see her dad hesitate for a moment, deciding whether or not to admit his own secret. But his vanity won out and he said, pretending to be casual, 'As it happens I'm an arch villain. I plot against super heroes, steal secret plans, and generally unleash mayhem on the city of Multiplicity.'

'What a coincidence,' Professor Vention giggled merrily. 'I'm in the same line of work. In fact, I'm currently enmeshed in a devious plan to manipulate the Multiverse.'

'You are?' Doctor D. Void was delighted. It seemed as if his truth serum was working. 'Did you hear that, Jewel? Professor Vention's a villain too.'

'I heard,' Jewel said. 'That's great, Dad.'

Luckily neither of the scientists noticed that she was a bit less than enthusiastic. Doctor D. Void was refilling Vention's glass. Soon the two men were competing to see who could tell the best stories of villainous schemes and dastardly plots they'd been involved in.

Jewel listened carefully. She didn't trust Professor Vention. When they'd been looking around the ship she'd mentioned the swirling lights she'd seen and he'd muttered something about 'side effects' of space travel and looked shifty.

'The worst of the job is those pesky heroes,' Doctor D. Void said. 'One of the reasons I'm exploring space is that it's hard work being a villain. No one ever writes about how cunning your plans were. They just interview those heroes over and over again and congratulate them for saving the day.'

'So true, so true.' Professor N. Vention looked wilder than ever and spilt his drink over himself in his eagerness to agree. 'Just when you've come up with a really excellent scheme, they stroll in and foil it in the nick of time. I used to have the same problem myself.'

'You certainly do,' the doctor agreed. 'But what do you mean, you *used* to have that problem. Was that before you moved to Planet X?'

'That's right.' The professor was looking smug again. 'But my being on Planet X is all part of the plan. I finally figured out a way to handle the heroes.'

'What is it?' The doctor was fascinated.

'If you can't beat them, join them!' Professor Vention announced grandly.

'Oh.' The doctor frowned. 'Then you made *peace*?' He didn't look at all impressed.

'No no no.' Professor Vention shook his head. 'It's not like that. In fact you could say they joined me. You see, super heroes love having power. I've persuaded them to join me in a scheme that will give them more power than ever before. But it's a scheme so devious they've had to become villains to do it. When the Infinity League is successful, I'll be in charge of the most villainous villains in any universe!'

'You will?' Doctor D. Void was very interested. 'How will you manage that?'

'Through sheer cunningness.' Professor Vention was beaming with delight at his own plan. 'I've invented a device called the Universal Equalizer. What it does is this . . .'

When Ben felt the hand on his shoulder he nearly screamed. Another hand covered his mouth before he could make a sound and the other Zeroes turned to stare at him.

'Why are you squirming about like that?' Pippa said. 'What's the matter?'

'He looks ill,' Marcus said.

'Say something,' Toby ordered. 'What's wrong?'

Ben felt the hand move away from his mouth and suddenly the other Zeroes all smiled, looking relieved. Before he turned round he already knew what he would see. The space behind him had been empty but now a woman with red hair was there.

'Fay,' he said. 'What are *you* doing here?'

'I followed the Hero Squad,' the woman explained. 'And then I spotted you. Come on, we'd better get off this saucer before it leaves.'

'Good plan,' Ben agreed.

Toby opened the door again and they hurried down the ramp. At the bottom Fay turned around and said, 'We'd better try and get this shut, or they'll guess something's up.'

It took all five of them to lift the ramp up from the ground but once they'd managed to get it over their heads there was a buzzing sound and it went the rest of the way automatically.

'What time is it?' Ben asked, suddenly worried by how long they'd spent in the ship.

'It's pretty late,' Toby said. 'You guys had better get back to the cinema before your parents come to pick you up. I'll phone you tomorrow, OK?'

'Better make it first thing in the morning,' Pippa warned. 'The Infinity League could send the signal any time.'

'And when they do all our parents will walk into that Equalizer thing,' Marcus added. 'And who knows what'll happen then.'

'I don't think they'll do anything tonight,' Fay told them. 'Apparently the Equalizer needs to draw power for at least twenty-four hours before it's ready to be switched on.'

'But what does it do?' Ben asked and Fay looked worried.

'I don't know,' she said.

When they got back to the cinema Ben's mum was outside talking to one of the ticket attendants. She looked very worried but when she saw Ben her face changed to being cross instead.

'Where did you go off to?' she demanded. 'I told you to meet me here!'

'I'm terribly sorry,' Fay said, stepping forward

so Ben's mum would see her. 'I met Ben and his friends in the cinema and offered to buy them an ice-cream from the shop around the corner after the film. I didn't realize we'd be gone so long.'

Ben's mum still looked a bit cross but it wasn't as if Fay was a stranger. She recognized her as Ben's dad's girlfriend, although of course she had no idea she was also the Fade.

'I see,' she said.

'I really am very sorry,' Fay continued. 'I should have waited and checked with you. I was just so pleased to see Ben.'

'That's OK, Fay,' Ben's mum said eventually. She wanted Ben to get on with Keith and Fay. Besides, it had been all right in the end. 'Well, Ben and I had better get home,' she said. 'It's late.'

It was very late by the time Ben got home. As he went to bed he saw that his phone had got four missed messages from Jewel, but taking a look at his mum's face he realized now would not be a good time to ask if he could make a phone call.

'I'll call her first thing in the morning,' he

decided as he finally fell asleep. 'If the Zeroes are going to beat the Infinity League we'll need her help. Although I don't know what she'll be able to do all the way out in space.'

It had only been a couple of days since Jewel had left but so much had happened that by the time they finally got to talk there was a lot to say. Toby called the others as he'd promised the next morning and once they were all connected, Ben got his phone to contact Jewel as well. The screen divided into four, showing Toby in the secret lair, Marcus at Animo's zoo, and Pippa at Power Towers. Each of the others could see Ben's room and they all waited as the fourth quarter of the screen changed from completely black to mostly black as Jewel appeared in her cabin on the spaceship Black Hole.

Jewel looked worried and relieved all at once as the other Zeroes appeared on the screen in front of her.

'I've been trying to get in touch with you since yesterday,' she said. 'There's something I need to tell you.'

'Us too,' Ben replied. 'Our parents are in big trouble and it's all because of some people who call themselves the Infinity League.'

'But that's what I was going to warn you about!' Jewel said. 'Dad and I met a mad scientist on Planet X and he's got a villainous scheme that's just awful. He's in charge of the Infinity League and he's invented something called the Universal Equalizer . . .'

'You know what it does?' Toby interrupted. 'We sneaked into the flying saucer last night and we heard the Infinity League talking about it.'

'The flying saucer?' Jewel looked confused.

'We'd better explain it from the beginning,' Pippa said.

'Then you can tell us what you've found out,' Marcus added.

'I'll start,' Ben said, taking charge. He realized if they all talked at once it'd take three times as long. 'It all began after Doctor D. Void's spaceship left . . .'

As Ben explained about the arrival of the flying saucer and described General Excellence, Quanta, and Mesmeron, Jewel listened silently but she nodded several times as if what they were saying made sense. Toby took over when he repeated what the Fade had told him about the hypnotism and Pippa described the strange room they'd found on the flying saucer. Finally Marcus told the story of what they'd heard while they were hiding and he remembered to mention something he'd thought was odd.

'I noticed at the time,' he said. 'Mesmeron's voice is a lot like my dad's and Quanta sounds like Princess Power.'

'General Excellence sounds like Captain Excelsior too,' Toby added.

'If we hadn't guessed from the things they were saying it would have been impossible to tell them apart,' Pippa agreed.

'But what does it mean?' Ben asked again. 'None of it seems to make any sense.'

'Yes it does,' Jewel said grimly. 'It does if you know there's more than one universe and that each one is almost identical to the others. Almost but not quite.'

The other Zeroes fell silent as Jewel explained what she'd discovered the day before.

'Professor N. Vention told Dad all about it,' she said. 'He's the mad scientist I mentioned. We met him on a planet no one knows about and didn't even exist here until Vention brought it to our universe. The whole of Planet X is like a spaceship and it travels from universe to universe using his Infinity machine. He's the one who invented the whole Infinity League plan and the brains behind the idea of the Universal Equalizer.'

'So what *are* they up to?' Ben asked and Jewel explained.

'Back in Vention's home universe General Excellence, Quanta, and Mesmeron used to be super heroes. But super powers weren't enough for them. They wanted more and more power and eventually they joined up with Vention to get it.'

'You mean, as if the Hero Squad had joined Doctor D. Void?' Toby asked and Jewel nodded.

'They never would,' Pippa said. 'Mum doesn't care that much about power.'

'I'm not so sure,' Marcus said. 'Dad was really pleased to be invited to join the Infinity League. They all were.'

'Hush,' said Ben. 'Jewel still hasn't told us the whole plan.'

'Well, how it works is that for every person in our world, there's a different version of them in another universe,' Jewel said. 'For example, Toby has red hair but in another universe he might have brown hair instead. Or my name is Jewel, but in another universe there might be someone just like me called something different, like Gemma.'

'Then that explains why we almost recognized all those different super heroes,' Toby said. 'The Zookeeper and Commander Extreme! They were from different universes.'

'And that's why General Excellence and the others sounded familiar,' Marcus added. 'They must be . . .'

'Versions of our own parents!' Pippa realized the truth at the same moment. 'I bet that's why they all wear masks. Underneath Quanta must look just like Mum!'

'And Mesmeron has powers over people the same way Animo has over animals,' Marcus added. 'Except Dad never forces animals to do anything bad.'

'I can't believe my dad might turn into someone like Excellence,' Ben said, sounding disgusted. 'But they did look awfully similar.'

'It's the same with my dad and Professor Vention,' Jewel explained. 'I'm sure he's a version of Doctor D. Void from an alternative universe.' She looked embarrassed. 'I know my dad's a villain,' she said. 'But he's honestly not all bad. He's never invented anything like the Universal Equalizer.'

'But you still haven't told us what it does,' Ben reminded her.

'Sorry!' Jewel blushed. 'It's supposed to add all the universes together. The Infinity League have built part of it in every universe they've visited and linked it up to Planet X. Once the Infinity League turn it on all the heroes in every universe will have their powers added together to make it work. Then it'll collapse all the universes together until there's just one. Theirs.'

'You're talking about the end of the world!' Toby realized.

'Not just the world,' Jewel replied. 'The end of our universe. General Excellence will have his powers and Captain Excelsior's and everyone else who's like him in all the other universes. The same thing will happen to the others and our parents won't exist any more, and neither will we.'

There was a long silence as the Zeroes thought about it. It was certainly a fiendish plan. Only an evil genius could have come up with it. The only problem was, it looked as if it would work. The Universal Equalizer was already built. All the Infinity League needed to do was send the signal and all the hypnotized heroes from every universe would do their work for them, thinking they were saving their own worlds when actually they'd be destroying them.

'What are we going to do?' Ben asked and Jewel shook her head.

'I don't know,' she said in a small voice. 'I've been worrying myself sick ever since I heard about it and I can't think of anything.'

'This is worse than Mum wearing pink,' Pippa agreed. 'I don't want her to turn into Quanta and I definitely don't want to turn into whoever I am in another universe. I bet she's a soppy girl who wears a bow in her hair.' She made a face.

'I don't care if the version of me in a different universe doesn't have asthma,' Marcus said. 'Or if he's good at sports. I want to go on being me.'

There was another silence and then Toby

suddenly spoke up. He'd been very quiet until now.

'I suppose my parents are just henchmen in the other universes,' he said. 'Since there's not a version of them important enough to be in the Infinity League. I suppose I'm the only one it doesn't make any difference to. So it doesn't really matter what'd happen to me.'

Ben was frowning while Toby spoke. Then he shook his head.

'Of course it matters,' he said. 'You should be proud there's no version of your parents involved in the Infinity League. It just shows how much the Infinity League care about power instead of people. The League are the ones who don't care what happens to all the normal people.'

'I suppose,' Toby said. 'After all, heroes and villains are all different. Normal people are the same everywhere and they don't have any powers.'

Now everyone felt depressed and they still didn't have a plan. At least most of them didn't. It took the other Zeroes a while to realize that Ben was smiling.

'Toby,' he said, 'you're a genius. I've just figured out how we can stop the Infinity League and all it will take is the power of Zero!'

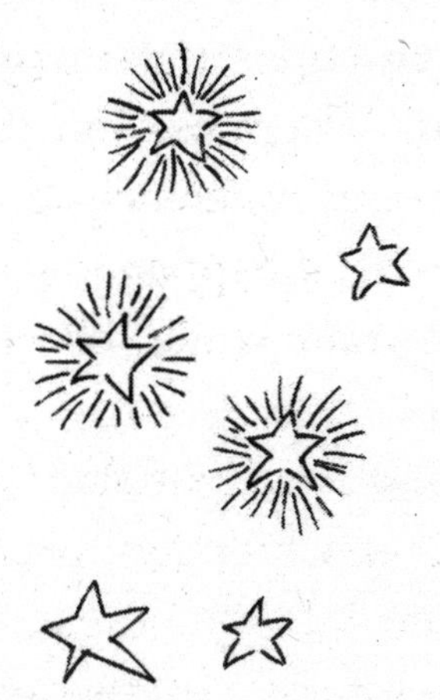

5
Zero Squared

When Ben explained his plan the other Zeroes started to smile. But there wasn't much time to lose. In less than twelve hours the Universal Equalizer would be turned on and then it would be too late for anyone to do anything.

After she'd hung up the phone Jewel went to find her father. She was going to have to be very careful what she said. But it was the only way to make her part of the plan work. She found him in the main observation room looking out at the grey rocky surface of Planet

X with the shining white laboratory facing him across the valley.

'Dad,' she said, 'I've been thinking about Professor Vention's plan and I don't think it's right . . .'

To her surprise her father nodded immediately.

'I agree!' he said. 'It's certainly not right.' Jewel couldn't believe it, but with her father's next sentence she understood. 'If anyone should be in charge of the universe's most villainous villains it's me. Me, Doctor Damian Void. Scourge of Multiplicity. Not some Johnny-Come-Lately who's never even been to a single criminals conference or one devious debate.'

'Um,' said Jewel. Then she smiled. 'You're right, Dad,' she said. 'He doesn't have anything like your experience with cunning plans. He'll probably get it all wrong anyway. It should be you standing on the Equalizer when the time comes.'

A slow smile spread across D. Void's face.

'I like that idea,' he said. 'But how to manage it?' He thought for a while and Jewel waited.

For her part of the plan to work someone had

to get Professor Vention out of the way. Her father might be a villain but he wasn't completely loopy. With him running the Equalizer, they had a chance. If Vention was in charge it would be a lot harder to pull off Ben's plan.

'We can't just walk into the base and zap him,' D. Void said thoughtfully. 'He's got all those robots protecting him. It's a pity I didn't think of this yesterday when he was on the ship.'

'Yes, Dad,' Jewel said, not mentioning that it had been her idea, not his.

'But my robots are just as good as his,' D. Void continued. 'If I can just get them to surround him . . .' He paused. 'Jewel,' he said, 'do we have any white paint on the ship?'

Jewel thought about it. There were stacks and stacks of black paint, of course.

'I don't know,' she said. 'But the robots could probably make some.'

'Go and tell them to make five gallons of it,' Doctor D. Void ordered. 'And then find some brushes. We've got lots of work ahead of us.'

Two hours later the doctor and Jewel were back in their spacesuits and walking towards Vention's laboratory. Following them were fifty white robots, shaped like a salt cellar or a pepper pot. Jewel was careful not to get too close to them: the paint was still a bit wet. As they reached the doors, the doctor turned to address the robots.

'Right,' he said. 'You know what to do. You've got ten minutes to find all of Vention's robots and zap them with your disruptor beams. Go!'

Jewel watched as the robots whizzed off down the corridors, beeping excitedly to each other. She and the doctor followed more slowly, walking quite calmly through the base. By the time they got to the control room with its walls covered in numbers and symbols Jewel was feeling confident.

'Good morning, Professor,' Doctor D. Void said as they walked into the room.

The professor was tinkering with the metal cage of the Infinity machine in the middle of the room and he looked irritated as they arrived.

'I don't have time to socialize,' he said. 'Today's the day I conquer every universe!'

'No,' said Doctor D. Void, drawing a ray gun. 'Today's the day *I* conquer every universe. You, I'm afraid, are going to be locked in your room.'

'What?' The professor couldn't believe it. 'What is this? Where's your loyalty to a fellow villain?'

'Villains don't have any loyalty,' Doctor D. Void said. 'We give the orders, we don't obey them.'

'You've made a mistake opposing me,' said Vention. Raising his voice he added: 'ROBOTS! ATTACK!'

Jewel almost felt sorry for him. The white robots that swarmed into the room came nowhere near her or her dad. Instead they surrounded Vention, beeping and pointing their grapplers at him threateningly.

Vention was furious. As the robots led him away he shouted back over his shoulder:

'I'll get even with you, D. Void . . . if it's the last thing I do!'

'Yes, yes.' The doctor didn't even turn his head. 'Whatever you say.' He was looking at the equipment with a gleam in his eye. Pointing out a large timer he said, 'Look, Jewel, it looks as if the machine's set to start up automatically at midnight tonight.'

'In that case you'd better check over Vention's plans,' Jewel said. 'Just in case he's got something wrong.'

'Good idea.' The doctor nodded and picked up a bundle of blueprints, taking them into an office to look at them in more detail.

Jewel waited until he was gone and then she went to one of the machines. It had a television screen and a whole row of buttons and a telephone handset attached to it. Picking up the telephone receiver, Jewel looked at the buttons. They were labelled and halfway down was one marked 'Gemma'. Crossing her fingers, Jewel pressed it and waited, trying not to bite her fingernails. Professor Vention had said he called home but his daughter always hung up on him. That meant he had a way to contact his original universe. She only hoped Gemma would listen.

Finally a girl appeared on the screen. She had long glossy black hair and green eyes, which widened as she saw Jewel.

'Hello, Gemma,' Jewel said quietly. 'Tell me, would you like to help stop the Infinity League's plan?'

Gemma Vention didn't even think for a moment.

'What do I have to do?' she asked.

Back on Earth Ben and Marcus were sneaking into Hero Heights together. This would have been impossible for almost anyone else but it was Marcus who'd helped his dad learn how the Hero Squad's security system worked and he remembered the passwords.

'All the same, I feel bad,' he told Ben as they tiptoed past Hero Squad cars and motorcycles in the garage and took the lift up to the top floor. 'Dad trusted me with that password. He didn't mean for me to use it to break in.'

'It's for their own good,' Ben reminded him. 'This is the only way.'

When they reached the top floor it wasn't

hard to find the Universal Equalizer. It was huge, taking up almost the whole control room. It was shaped like a cage or a climbing frame, large enough for three people to stand inside it.

'I wish we could just smash it,' Marcus said.

'Trust me,' Ben told him. 'This way is better. Even if we smashed this one, there are still all the others in the other universes. We have to make sure to break them all at once.'

'I know,' Marcus said. 'All the same it gives me the creeps.'

'Well, let's get this over with,' Ben told him. Taking out his video phone he held it ready. 'Are you sure this will work?'

'This thing's already connected to the other universes,' Marcus said. 'So there's already a connection. But I can't be sure until we try it.'

He opened the tool box he had brought with him and took out some different kinds of cables and began to attach them, some to Ben's phone, some to the Universal Equalizer and the rest to the computer consoles around the control room. Every now and then he'd ask Ben to pass him a screwdriver or hold a wire while he climbed under a console to find the right power socket. Soon the entire room was a spider's web of cables and wires.

Ben stood in the middle, holding his phone and waiting. Finally Marcus stopped crawling around the floor.

'It's ready,' he said. 'You might feel a little electric shock though.'

Ben nodded and began to press buttons on his phone, telling it to dial five numbers at once: Pippa's at Power Towers, Jewel's on the Black Hole, Toby's at the secret lair, and then finally Marcus's at the zoo and his own number. As he punched in the last number he gritted his teeth and then pressed the green button to make a connection.

There was a jolt of electricity and Ben nearly dropped the phone. He could actually see the power sizzling across the cage of the Universal Equalizer and along the cables around the room. The whole control room filled with a loud ringing sound, echoing from wall to wall, as the phone tried to make a connection.

Suddenly one of the hundreds of screens came to life and Marcus pointed at it excitedly.

There was a boy who looked just like Ben, except for the fact he was dressed in different clothes. His expression was surprised and he opened his mouth to speak. But before he could say anything the next screen turned on. It was a boy who looked a lot like Marcus except that he was dressed in a sports kit and looked a lot stronger for his age. He stared at them from the screen and at the first boy, looking completely amazed.

The next screen turned on a second later. Ben and Marcus exchanged grins when they saw it was a girl dressed in a ruffled pink dress with a pink bow in her hair. A second later a red-headed boy appeared on another screen and a girl with short spikey black hair. But that wasn't the last of them. The Infinity League had visited over fifty different worlds and left a part of the Universal Equalizer on each of them. Now Marcus had connected Ben's phone to all those universes and Zeroes from every one of them were appearing on screens throughout the room.

There were fat Zeroes and skinny Zeroes, tall Zeroes, short Zeroes, Zeroes who looked friendly, and Zeroes who looked annoyed. Ben saw his own face reflected all around the room, wearing every possible expression. Marcus saw himself as an athlete, with a cat, with a parrot, with a robotic dog with glowing green eyes. There were Pippas in dresses, Pippas with bows in their hair, Pippas completely covered in mud, and Pippas smiling sweetly and innocently as well as ones with the fiendish grin they recognized. Most of the Tobys were strong and muscled but Marcus spotted one who looked weedy and Ben saw one in a ballet costume. Almost all the Jewels were pretty, but some looked confident and others seemed shy.

It was weird to see them all at once: universe after universe of Zeroes. In fact, Ben thought, they probably weren't all Zeroes since maybe in some of those other universes they'd never actually met each other and formed the Super Zeroes club. But that was about to change.

'Hello, everyone,' he said, feeling a bit nervous with so many people listening to him. When he'd suggested trying to contact the Zeroes in other universes it had made sense. Jewel was supposed to be finding the five from the Infinity League's universe and Ben and

Marcus had agreed to make a connection with all the others from the places the Infinity League had been before. Toby and Pippa's job was the most difficult of all. Could they pull it off?

But the problem was that although the children on the screen were all watching him, a lot of them didn't look pleased to be called up. Ben was remembering how he had felt about super heroes and saving the world and realized that he couldn't make a big speech telling them what to do. But maybe he could ask them.

'My name's Ben Carter,' he said. 'I'm calling you up because my friends and I found out about something you should all know. Because although we're all different we've all got something in common.'

'A lot of us look really like each other,' said one of the Tobys. 'Is that what you mean?'

'Like each other but in a weird way,' said one of the Pippas and crossed her eyes at another one.

'This is something about super heroes, isn't it?' one of the Bens said, looking suspicious.

'It is,' he said carefully. 'And about villains. But most importantly it's about normal people and about how important we are.'

Now he really had their attention. The ones who'd been pulling faces at each other started to look more serious and the ones who'd looked bored or annoyed before seemed more friendly.

'What makes us different is that we're all from different universes,' Ben went on. 'And the thing we have in common is we all know someone who's a hero or a villain and sometimes we don't get noticed because people are impressed by flashy costumes and poses. The thing you need to know about is something called the Infinity League who are like the worst parts of heroes and villains put together.'

'I know who you mean,' said one of the Marcuses. 'They were here in my universe.' He looked around and seemed to recognize a nearby Pippa and waved to her. 'In our universe, I mean. They claimed to be heroes.'

'If my father's involved in this they're certainly not heroes,' said one of the Jewels. 'What are this Infinity League up to and why are you telling us about it?'

'Because we need your help,' Ben explained. It would be all right, he realized. He could convince the Zeroes. This would work after all.

As quickly as he could he repeated everything he knew of the Infinity League's plan and about what was supposed to happen at midnight tonight when all the heroes went to their versions of the Universal Equalizer.

'They want to add all the universes together to make themselves more powerful,' he explained. 'But they don't care how it'll affect all the normal people. If our universes are added together there won't be lots of us. Instead there'll be new people, made up of the bits the Infinity League think are the best.'

Everyone looked worried now but Ben could see they trusted him and so he told them the plan.

'My friend Jewel will have control of the machine tonight,' he said. 'She's on Planet X, which is the tenth planet in the solar system. At midnight Planet X will exist in every universe at once as the Universal Equalizer tries to add everyone together.'

Ben took a deep breath. Remembering how Jewel had explained it to him earlier, he went on.

'The Equalizer's supposed to draw power from all the different heroes, connecting them all together and then collapsing everything into one universe. But if there's no one to draw power from, the Equalizer won't be able to add our universes together and it'll be the Infinity League that collapses. So we've got to find a way of keeping the heroes away from the Equalizer when it's turned on.'

The Zeroes from all the other universes were listening silently and Marcus, watching the screens, saw that some of them were taking notes. Ben was smiling as he announced his idea:

'So our plan is that tonight there should be conflict between the heroes and the villains in every universe. We need robot rampages, we need mutant menaces, we need hordes of henchmen, anything and everything that'll keep the heroes distracted.'

There was silence for a moment and then everyone began talking at once. It took Ben and Marcus a minute to realize what was happening. All the children were trying to identify the Zeroes from their own universe and making arrangements to meet up. In fact, they were all having different versions of the conversation Ben and his friends had had when they first met.

None of them had said no. Instead they were all working out what they could do to help each other.

Ben beamed; he'd always known he could count on his friends. Now all the different versions of him would have friends too.

'I think they'll do it,' he said to Marcus.

'I think so too,' Marcus nodded. 'But it's going to take them a while to make plans. Meanwhile . . .'

'Toby and Pippa have to make sure the plan works *here*.'

Toby and Pippa were in Doctor D. Void's secret lair. Luckily Pippa, with her black clothes and pen and ink tattoos and her confident attitude fitted right in with the henchmen. There were a lot of henchmen. Terry and Tina Tench had started advertising as soon as the Infinity League had turned up. Now the lair was almost bursting with lizardmen and mechanoids and all sorts of people in weird costumes. Hero costumes were ridiculous enough but a villain's sidekicks and musclemen had to wear uniforms that made them look scary.

As they walked through the crowd Pippa had to bite her tongue to stop herself giggling. Apparently one woman thought she'd look really frightening if she dressed up in huge purple butterfly wings and these kept banging into people as she walked. There was a man dressed as a walrus, or perhaps a walrus dressed as a man. There were a whole group of acrobats forming a human pyramid and Pippa nudged Toby and said, 'They're better at that than we were.'

'Where do you think I got the idea from?' Toby grinned.

Toby and Pippa had to keep moving because they were spreading a rumour. It was too difficult for Toby to explain directly to his parents why they needed to make trouble for the Hero Squad tonight. Instead they'd decided to spread the rumour through the henchmen.

'What was that you said, Power Girl?' said Toby loudly as they paused by a group of sidekicks.

'I said I heard the Hero Squad would be going into space tonight,' Pippa replied. 'The city will be practically unprotected.'

They waited until the sidekicks had started whispering among themselves and then moved on to another group.

'What was that, Wonder Boy?' Pippa asked. 'You really think tonight's the best time to take over?'

'Definitely, everyone's talking about how the Hero Squad will be away. Only a fool would miss this opportunity,' Toby replied.

A minute later they were on to the next group. Before long they weren't even having to start the rumour themselves. All over the base people were looking at each other and saying:

'Tonight?'

'That's what I heard . . .'

'. . . Hero Squad away . . .'

'We shouldn't miss this chance.'

'At midnight, you said?'

Toby and Pippa grinned at each other. The plan was working. Tonight there would be a crime wave like nothing Multiplicity had ever seen.

'I hope the Hero Squad can handle it,' Pippa said, remembering how they had started off a robot rampage once before and it hadn't gone exactly to plan. 'If they can't we'll have caused a lot of trouble.'

'Well.' Toby looked a bit shamefaced. 'If the villains do well it'll be good for my parents. I wouldn't mind if the Hero Squad didn't catch *all* the people we've sent.'

That night, as it started to get dark, the villains began their campaign. Up in Hero Heights the Hero Squad had been waiting for the Infinity League's signal when they got the news. Suddenly reports were coming in all over town about things they were needed to help with. It wasn't one big plan, like the usual villainous scheme. Instead it was all sorts of strange small plans at once.

A villain called the cat burglar had played a magic whistle and got all the cats in Multiplicity to climb the trees in the city park. Now the park was full of fire engines and ladders and little old ladies calling out things like: 'Be careful, Snookums scratches!' Meanwhile a team of goons called the Bonfire Bunch had set fire to the arboretum and none of the fire engines could get there in time.

A motley crew of musclemen had met up at the Multiplicity museum with earth-moving machinery and had stolen the whole building and were driving off with it down the motorway. A woman with purple wings was swarming around the city in a cloud of moths and insects, chasing people and batting at them with a giant people-swatter. Someone called the Walrus had taken over the city's main seafood restaurant and was demanding serving after serving of shellfish.

There were robots rampaging up and down the streets, the power kept going on and off, traffic jams were creating chaos, and the sewers were overflowing with green goo and orange ooze and every shade of slime imaginable.

As soon as one of the heroes set off to sort out one of the problems, another problem would arrive. After dashing in and out for a while, eventually Captain Excelsior, Animo, and

Princess Power switched on their answerphone and left the building together.

'If the Infinity League call us tonight they'll have to wait,' Captain Excelsior said.

'It's tough enough work protecting this city,' Animo agreed.

'Do you ever get the feeling there's something we're missing?' Princess Power asked. 'Something that's almost right in front of us?'

'Let's just get out there and do our job,' Captain Excelsior declared and the three of them swooped off into the night.

Once they were gone, a shadow moved in the corner of the room as a woman appeared out of nowhere. The Fade had been watching Hero Heights all day and when Ben and Marcus had left she'd tidied up a few pieces of cabling they'd missed. It was nearly midnight now, almost time. In the middle of the room the Universal Equalizer started to glow with an eerie swirling light.

Fay didn't know what Jewel was planning, far away on Planet X. Whatever it was, she hoped it worked.

* * *

Jewel's plan had worked a little too well. She'd used the idea of taking over the Equalizer to convince her father to help to get rid of Vention. But she'd made a mistake when she'd suggested that he become the most villainous villain in any universe.

Professor N. Vention was locked safely away but Doctor D. Void was now striding up and down through the massed hordes of robots, some white and some now rather more streaky grey.

'This will be the beginning of a brave new era,' he said. 'When I have the knowledge of multiple versions of me I will be the most intelligent man in the universe. I will run a scientific society than spans the stars.'

The robots beeped excitedly. It didn't seem to make any difference to them who was in charge. Jewel wondered if they could even tell the difference between Vention and Void. She was beginning to worry that she couldn't either.

High above them through the transparent roof Jewel could see the stars, pinpoints of white light of distant suns. As the time crept towards midnight on Earth, Planet X would exist in multiple universes at once and she wondered if

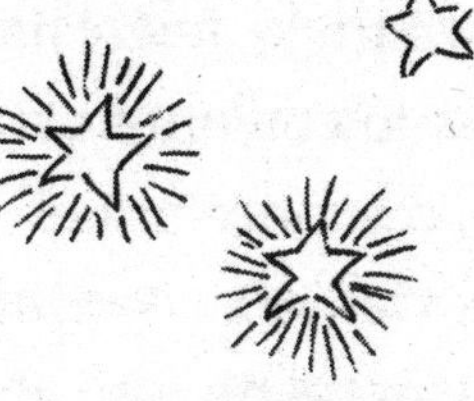
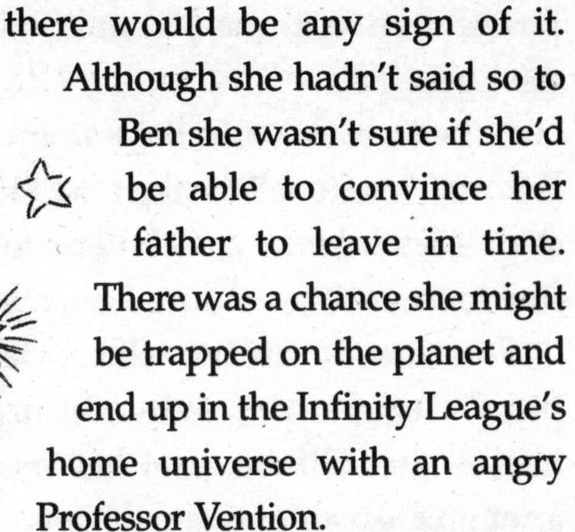

there would be any sign of it. Although she hadn't said so to Ben she wasn't sure if she'd be able to convince her father to leave in time. There was a chance she might be trapped on the planet and end up in the Infinity League's home universe with an angry Professor Vention.

If the Zeroes plan succeeded the Equalizer wouldn't work. But the strange cage in the middle of the room was glowing with a weird light. It was a light that was all sorts of colours at once. The Equalizer was getting its power from somewhere.

The strange light spiralled round and round the cage, looping like an infinity sign and Jewel thought about the conversation she'd had with Gemma Vention.

'This is why I wouldn't come with my dad to Planet X,' Gemma had explained. 'The planet's unstable—just like my dad. He's been using the super powers of the Infinity League like a fuel to take Planet X from universe to universe. If the power runs out, the planet could collapse like the Equalizer.'

'If Ben's plan works the Infinity League will be the only ones to fall for their own trick,' Jewel had said. 'I don't know if I'll be able to convince your dad to leave. I'm not sure I can convince mine.'

'I've already tried to tell my dad it's a terrible plan,' Gemma said sadly. 'In my universe the heroes are villains and no one cares about anything except power. If my father and the Infinity League are added together it won't make any difference. But I hope you can convince your father to get out.'

Jewel stepped back from the cage shape of the Infinity machine and turned to her father.

'Dad,' she said slowly, 'now you're in charge of the Infinity League, right? The ones who've been out there persuading super heroes across the multiverse to use the Equalizer.'

'I suppose so.' Doctor D. Void was frowning up at the night sky, which had started to shimmer with a swirling coloured light. 'I suppose I might have a fight on my hands when they find out Vention's not in charge any more. They sound like a troublesome trio.'

'They're like the Hero Squad, aren't they?' Jewel pointed out. 'Only villainous, and soon they'll have the combined powers of all the heroes from different universes as well.'

'Yeees.' D. Void was starting to look worried. The light from the machine was getting brighter and the shadows getting darker and he could feel the floor shaking slightly beneath his feet. 'Now I come to think of it Vention never did say how he planned to keep them in line.'

'I think maybe he was a bit carried away with his invention,' Jewel said, looking pointedly at the swirling lines of equations that covered the walls, spiralling into the vast infinity sign. 'Mad scientists are like that.'

Doctor D. Void looked around the room at the numbers and symbols written across all the walls. He looked at the swirling lights of the Infinity machine and the rows of salt-and-pepper-pot robots beeping together in a jangling victory song. He turned his head to look up at the sickly light that spanned the sky from horizon to horizon; then down to look at the vibrating metal plates of the floor.

'So,' Jewel said. 'Is the plan working? Do you feel your intelligence growing?'

Doctor D. Void looked at his daughter. Then he looked at the countdown. Then he looked at the robots who were humming nervously as they felt the ground shake.

'Yes,' he said, 'I do. And I've made a decision. Vention can keep his Planet X and his Universal Equalizer and his plan. But . . .' he looked suddenly resolute, 'I'm taking his robots.'

'Good plan, Dad,' Jewel said. The robots beeped agreement. 'I think we had better start running now.'

'Even better plan . . .' said the doctor, handing her the helmet of her spacesuit.

Arch villains don't normally run. But if your loyal army of robots panics and picks you up and carries you back to your ship, you may as well sit back and enjoy the ride. The robots seemed to have been learning something from their recent experiences. The zebra-striped ones were showing the new group how to anchor themselves to the deck with magnets while Doctor D. Void ran to the pilot's seat.

As the spaceship lifted off Jewel could see the

sensor image of Planet X blurring behind trailing ripples and ribbons of colour.

'What's happening to it?' she asked.

'The fabric of space is shredding.' Doctor D. Void was studying the readouts on his screens as he frantically punched buttons and pulled the levers of the Black Hole's controls. 'The Equalizer isn't drawing enough power to keep it in every universe at once. The Infinity League can't have persuaded anyone to stand on the Equalizer at all.'

As the blurred colours merged together the image of the planet faded and before long it was gone, leaving nothing behind but the blackness of space.

'Well done, Dad,' Jewel said. 'You really are better than Vention. And you got us away just in time. The planet's gone.'

'It's probably been sucked back to the universe it came from,' D. Void said, finally relaxing. 'Either that or . . .'

'Or?' Jewel crossed her fingers, thinking of Gemma Vention.

'Assuming the Infinity League were the only ones to be standing in the right place, instead of giving them the combined powers of every universe, they might be divided, creating many more universes in which they were just normal . . .'

'I hope that's true,' Jewel said. In the end neither she nor Gemma had been sure what would happen. But she'd asked Gemma to promise that whatever happened, she'd seek out the other Zeroes in her world, because if there was anyone who wouldn't be impressed by special powers, it was them.

Suddenly she missed her own friends very badly. Her father was looking rather exhausted, as he always did after a nefarious plan had gone wrong. Only the robots seemed cheerful. Jewel was starting to wonder what it was they were really saying with all those beeps. She was starting to realize quite how much variation there was to it.

She beeped a couple of times experimentally to herself and a couple of the robots turned to look at her. Every now and then one of her father's inventions really did work and she wondered if it was possible the robots could have developed their own language.

Doctor D. Void was tapping the controls thoughtfully, as a robot glided up with a tea tray.

'All the problems with Vention's plan makes me wonder what's happening at home,' he said. 'I was never entirely sure about leaving Tench in charge. He'd better not have been slacking on the job.'

'The Infinity League will have visited Multiplicity as well,' Jewel reminded him.

'What do you say to going back?' the doctor said. 'We've already discovered a planet and the secrets of multiverse travel. And I've thought of at least five new nefarious schemes.' He beamed, and Jewel sighed. Some things never changed.

Then she giggled, as a robot offered Dr Void a spoonful of cat-hair to stir into his tea.

One week later all the Zeroes were together again. When the Universal Equalizer had been turned on it had glowed brightly for a while and then blown up spectacularly in a hail of bolts and screws and burning circuitry. According to Marcus the Hero Squad were still clearing bits of it out of their control room.

'They don't remember anything about being hypnotized,' Marcus said. 'But my dad said the other day that he was glad the Infinity League didn't need him after all. All the trouble in the city has convinced him he's got enough to do here.'

'Mum's the same,' Pippa agreed. 'She said she knew there was something odd about Quanta all along.'

'The only one who knew anything was Fay,' Ben said. 'By the way, she asked me to tell you guys that she owes us an ice-cream. I thought we'd wait until Jewel was back though.'

Jewel smiled at them.

'I really missed you lot,' she said. 'When you were all breaking into the flying saucer I thought you were all having fun and couldn't be bothered to answer the phone.'

'No way,' Ben said. 'We couldn't have done it without you. Without all of us.'

'Yeah,' Toby said. 'I have to admit I was worried for a while there. Especially when Pippa and I were trying to convince the henchmen to attack.'

'My dad thought that was brilliant though,' Jewel told him. 'He's really impressed at the amount of mayhem the henchmen caused in just a week. He was talking about giving your dad a raise.'

'He should do,' Toby agreed. 'With all those robots running around the lair. The way they beep at each other all the time is even noisier than the cats!'

Ben was thinking about the Zeroes from the other universes and wondering if he'd ever see them again. With the Universal Equalizer destroyed, he hadn't had a way to contact them and say thank you. Friends were supposed to look out for you, help you out with the tricky bits of your homework, and phone you up when you needed to talk. But the Zeroes from other universes had helped without knowing him at all. He hoped that, wherever they were, they knew they'd made a difference.

Suddenly Ben grinned. Thinking about homework had reminded him of something.

'You know,' he said, 'the Infinity League never did have a chance. I just remembered something our maths teacher told us. Zero times infinity is still zero.'

'I guess Professor Vention never did that sum,' Jewel agreed, 'or he'd know that there are people who don't need or want super powers.'

'People who just want to lead a normal life,' Ben agreed. 'Speaking of which, who else wants an ice cream?'